Wendel and The Great One

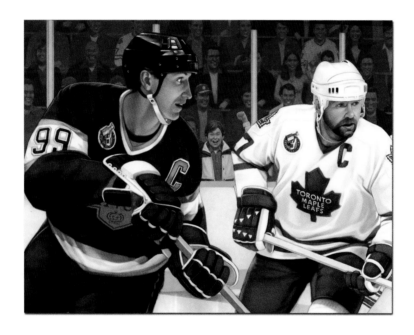

Mike Leonetti

illustrations by
Greg Banning

Scholastic Canada Ltd.
Toronto New York London Auckland Sydney
Mexico City New Delhi Hong Kong Buenos Aires

ACKNOWLEDGEMENTS

The books of the following authors were used to research this story: Howard Berger, Canadian Press (editors), John Davidson, Dan Diamond, Bob Ferguson, Trent Frayne, Don Gillmor, Wayne Gretzky, Peter Gzowski, Janet Lunn, Elizabeth MacLeod, Christopher Moore, Rick Reilly, Rick Sadowski, Michael Ulmer, Barry Wilner and Scott Young. Magazines reviewed: *Hockey Illustrated*, *Hockey News*, Toronto Maple Leafs game day programs from the 1992–93 season. Newspapers consulted: *Globe and Mail, The Toronto Star, Toronto Sun.* Video/Films reviewed: *1993 Stanley Cup, The Passion Returns: 1992–93 Maple Leafs, Hockey Night in Canada*'s original broadcasts of games six and seven of the Leafs/Kings playoff series, TSN rebroadcast of game seven featuring interviews with Wendel Clark and Wayne Gretzky. Reference Books: Toronto Maple Leafs media guides, 1992–94 and 1993–94, *National Hockey League Official Guide and Record Book 1993–94*, as well as 1990–2000 issues.

Scholastic Canada Ltd.
604 King Street West, Toronto, Ontario M5V 1E1, Canada

Scholastic Inc.
557 Broadway, New York, NY 10012, USA

Scholastic Australia Pty Limited
PO Box 579, Gosford, NSW 2250, Australia

Scholastic New Zealand Limited
Private Bag 94407, Botany, Manukau 2163, New Zealand

Scholastic Children's Books
Euston House, 24 Eversholt Street, London NW1 1DB, UK

Library and Archives Canada Cataloguing in Publication
Leonetti, Mike, 1958-
Wendel and the great one / by Mike Leonetti ; illustrated by Greg Banning.

ISBN 978-0-545-98069-2

1. Clark, Wendel, 1966- —Juvenile fiction. 2. Gretzky, Wayne, 1961-
—Juvenile fiction. I. Banning, Greg II. Title.
PS8573.E58734W45 2010   jC813'.54   C2010-901781-1

6 5 4 3 2 1   Printed in Singapore 46   10 11 12 13

Hockey practice had ended and we all clomped our way back into the locker room. We were about to change out of our uniforms when Coach Graves made a surprise announcement.

"Listen up, guys," he said, passing out bits of paper. "Today we're going to pick a captain. Everyone gets a vote. Think about it carefully. I'll count the votes and tell you who gets to put the C on his sweater."

After a few minutes, we had finished voting. I voted for Adam, our best player.

A moment later, Coach Graves walked over to me and said, "Congratulations, David! You're captain of the Raiders!"

I couldn't believe it! All the guys came over and gave me high-fives or patted me on the back. I just sat there, not knowing what to say.

When my dad picked me up after practice, I told him the news.

"Wow, David! It's a great honour to be voted captain of a team," he said.

"I know, but what does a captain do? How am I supposed to act? What should I say in the locker room? How do I lead?" I asked.

"Slow down, David," he said. "You should probably do some research on other captains. You can always learn by watching the best."

Dad was right. Watching captains in the NHL was sure to help me learn to become a better leader. In fact, my two favourite players were captains. One was Wendel Clark of the Toronto Maple Leafs. The other was the player I admired most: Wayne Gretzky of the Los Angeles Kings.

I had rookie cards for both Wendel and Gretzky, and had posters of each of them in my room. It would be great if I could be a captain just like them!

Toronto was my favourite team in the NHL, and Wendel Clark was one of the best players for the Maple Leafs. He had a wicked wrist shot and could throw some great body checks. The Leafs were hoping he would lead them back to the playoffs. He was a fan favourite. In Toronto he was known simply as "Wendel."

When Wendel was made captain of the Leafs he said, "I have the same sweater as everybody else; mine just has a letter on it." Wendel was a player who respected what the coach said and never complained.

Wayne Gretzky was the best player in the NHL. When he played for the Edmonton Oilers, they won the Stanley Cup four times. He held lots of NHL records and was a player who gave his all in every game. Now that he was with the Los Angeles Kings, he was making that team a top contender for the Cup. Everyone called him "The Great One."

Gretzky liked to make sure that his teammates got credit when they did something important. Even though he was the greatest star in hockey, he wanted to be treated like any other player. He worked hard and made sure he played his very best.

In our first game after I was named captain, we won a close one 3–2.
I helped with a goal and an assist. But we nearly lost the game when one
of our players made a big mistake. Nikolai was a great skater and could shoot
the puck hard, but he was new to Canada and didn't always understand
what the coach said. Luckily, our goalie made a great stop to save the game.

Afterward, Coach Graves called me into his office.

"David, now that you're captain, you need to make sure everyone feels like
part of the team. You know that Nikolai sometimes doesn't understand, so
maybe he doesn't feel like he's part of the team yet. You have to figure out
how to help him feel included, okay?"

"I'll try," I said. "But I'm not really sure what to do. He's sort of shy, and
I don't always know what he's saying."

"You'll figure it out," he said. "You should also watch other captains in our
league. You might learn something by watching how kids your age handle
being a leader."

I nodded, but I was still very unsure about the whole captain thing.

The next day at school, I spoke to my teacher, Mrs. Sartor, hoping she might be able to help me.

"Why don't you do your report about great Canadian leaders?" she said. "You can research people in sports, but you should look up others, as well."

It sounded like a good idea, so I went to the school library to start my report.

I found lots of examples of great Canadian leaders. In sports, there was Jean Beliveau, who used his skill and competitiveness to captain the Montreal Canadiens to five Stanley Cups. A brave girl named Marilyn Bell swam across Lake Ontario when nobody thought it could be done. Nancy Greene showed that perseverance paid off in becoming a world-champion skier.

A young athlete named Terry Fox was determined to run across Canada with just one good leg to raise money for vital research. Rick Hansen manoeuvred his wheelchair around the world to raise awareness about spinal cord injuries. Champion sprinter Harry Jerome used his fame to start fitness programs in schools and to promote rights for visible minorities.

There were many other examples of leadership outside of sports. Canada's best prime ministers had great leadership skills. Sir John A. Macdonald proved that compromise works, while Sir Wilfrid Laurier led the country by believing that Canada would grow and prosper. Lester Pearson persuaded the entire world that peace was possible, while Pierre Trudeau challenged Canadians to take control of their own destiny.

Cairine Wilson always stood up for what she believed and became the first female senator in Canada. Emily Stowe excelled in school to become the first female doctor in Canada. Roberta Bondar showed great initiative in science and went on to become the first Canadian woman in space.

I presented my report to the class. Mrs. Sartor said I did very well.

"Did this help you?" she asked.

"Yes," I said. "I learned a lot about the skills a leader needs. I really think it'll help me to be a good captain," I said.

Our team was beginning to play well, but I knew it would be great for us if we could get Nikolai more involved. One day after practice I got a few of the guys to help me work with Nikolai. Because he was such a good skater we worked on a play to spring him free for a shot on net. We explained everything to him carefully, making sure he understood us, and we kept practising.

Soon Nikolai started scoring a few goals. He would even joke around with everyone.

One day, I hung around the arena after practice to watch a game between two other teams in our league. The captains couldn't have been more different. One was very loud, barking at his teammates and even yelling at the officials. He would stand at the bench like he had to jump on the ice for every shift and take over the game.

The other captain encouraged his teammates every shift, whether he was on the ice or on the bench. He worked hard each time he was out on the ice. At the end of the game he had a chance to score into an empty net, but instead passed the puck to a teammate who didn't have many goals.

As captain, the one thing I decided to do was to encourage my players. It didn't always work, but we got better, and by the end of the year you could tell that Nikolai felt like a part of the team.

We made the playoffs but lost to the Steelers in overtime. Their captain set a good example for everyone. He wasn't the best player on his team, but he worked hard in his own end, helping out his goalie. When they gave him the champions' trophy, he quickly handed it to the teammate who had scored the winning goal. Later, when a team photo was being snapped, he made sure that everybody on the team was in the picture. You could see that they all looked up to him.

After the game, Coach Graves said, "You've come a long way as captain, David, and if you're captain next year, I'm sure you'll do an even better job. Just remember that you're always being watched for the example you set."

"I know, Coach," I said. "I've learned a lot this year just by watching some of the pros. I think I'll be better next season, too."

Even though I'd learned a lot about leadership from watching captains in my own league, there was nothing like watching pros like Wendel Clark and Wayne Gretzky lead their teams.

The Maple Leafs were having a great season under their new coach, Pat Burns. My dad had season tickets, so I went to many of the games. I loved to watch Wendel, Doug Gilmour, Dave Andreychuk and a young goalie named Felix Potvin. The team set a club record with 99 points and then beat Detroit and St. Louis in the first rounds of the playoffs. Wendel was playing the best hockey of his career, even though he was under great pressure to lead the team.

Gretzky missed much of the year because of an injury, but he came back to lead his team into the postseason. He got 65 points in only 45 games and then helped the Kings get past Calgary and Vancouver in the playoffs. That meant that the Maple Leafs and the Kings would meet in the next round to decide who would go to the finals!

I went to the first game of the series. It was awesome! The Leafs broke the game open with three goals in the final period to win 4–1. At the end of the game, Wendel stood up for Gilmour after he was checked roughly. As Wendel came to his teammate's defence, the crowd cheered wildly.

In the next game, Gretzky set up the winning goal to give the Kings a 3–2 win. The teams each won a game in Los Angeles, but the Leafs won the fifth game at home in overtime to put them within one game of winning the series.

The next game, in Los Angeles, was on television late at night. Luckily there was no school the next day, so I stayed up to watch it. Wendel did just about everything he could to get the Leafs a win. He scored a goal in the second period to give Toronto a 2–1 lead when he lifted a backhand shot over the Kings goalie. Even though Clark worked hard, the Leafs trailed 4–2 in the third period.

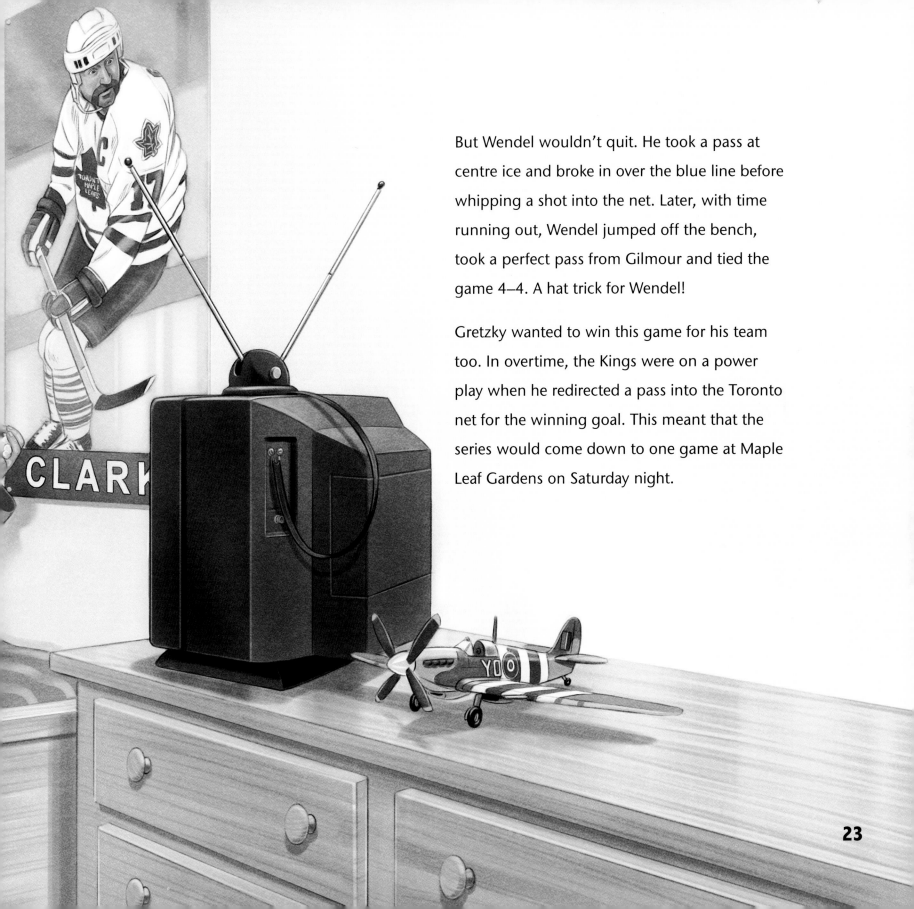

But Wendel wouldn't quit. He took a pass at centre ice and broke in over the blue line before whipping a shot into the net. Later, with time running out, Wendel jumped off the bench, took a perfect pass from Gilmour and tied the game 4–4. A hat trick for Wendel!

Gretzky wanted to win this game for his team too. In overtime, the Kings were on a power play when he redirected a pass into the Toronto net for the winning goal. This meant that the series would come down to one game at Maple Leaf Gardens on Saturday night.

The last game is one I'll never forget. We got to the Gardens early and took our seats. You could feel the excitement in the crowd. We were hoping to see Toronto make it to the finals for the first time since 1967! The game was also going to be a showdown between the two captains.

Wayne Gretzky said that Maple Leaf Gardens was a very special place for him: he had watched his first NHL game there with his grandmother when he was six years old. He loved to play in Toronto. On this night he opened the scoring when he took a pass off his skate on a two-on-one rush while his team was short-handed. He set up another goal to give the Kings a 2–0 lead.

Wendel got the Leafs going in the second period when he slammed home a pass from behind the net to make it 2–1. The Leafs tied it 2–2, but then Gretzky got himself free with the puck just inside the Toronto blue line. He fired a shot to beat Potvin and gave his team a 3–2 lead.

Wendel was playing as hard as he ever had; he seemed to be everywhere! Early in the third period he took a pass from Gilmour and tied the game 3–3! The crowd went wild, and it looked like the Leafs might be able to win it after all.

With less than five minutes to go, the Kings rushed into the Leafs end. The puck bounced to a Kings player who scored, giving them the lead. But there was still time for the Leafs to come back. Then Gretzky got the puck. As he circled around the Toronto net, he threw the puck out in front and it went into the net off a skate. Three goals for The Great One!

The Leafs didn't quit and even scored another goal. They stormed around the Kings' net in the final minute of the game, but the clock ran out. Los Angeles won the game 5–4 and would play Montreal for the Stanley Cup. Gretzky leapt off the bench and pumped his arms in celebration while Wendel skated away with his head down, upset that his team had lost.

The two captains shook hands and patted each other on the back. They had both played their hearts out.

On the way home Dad said to me, "Well, what did you think of the captains?"

I was still a bit down about the Leafs losing, but I said, "Wendel and Gretzky were incredible. They both showed how a captain leads with his actions on the ice."

"So after all your research, have you learned anything?" Dad asked.

"Leaders have to be determined. They have to listen to and include others, but they need to take charge. And they know that action is more important than talk."

"This was a great series to show how leadership can be so important to a team," said Dad.

"Yeah, it was. I learned that a leader never quits. Wendel never let the pressure keep him from doing his best. And Gretzky never stopped believing he could play better — no matter how well he played — until the game was over."

"It sounds like you want to be a captain more than ever," said Dad.

"Next year I'm going to be an even better captain. I'll just remind myself of how Wendel and The Great One, and all those other amazing Canadians, have shown us how to be great leaders!"

A NOTE TO THE READER

The names of many prominent Canadian leaders in various fields are mentioned in this book. We hope that all readers, especially young students, will take the time to learn more about their inspiring stories which have helped to shape the past, present and future of this great country.

ABOUT WENDEL CLARK

Wendel Clark was born in Kelvington, Saskatchewan, in 1966. After a stellar junior career with the Saskatoon Blades, he was selected first overall by the Toronto Maple Leafs in the 1985 Entry Draft. He took the NHL by storm in his first year by scoring 34 goals (a Leaf rookie record) and playing a bruising style of game. He was named to the NHL's all-rookie team for 1985–86, and by 1991 he was made the 14th captain in Leaf history. Clark played his best hockey with Toronto during the 1993 playoffs when he had 10 goals and 20 points in 21 games. He scored a career-high 46 goals for the Leafs in 1993–94 but was dealt to Quebec at the end of that season. The Leafs re-acquired Clark twice more before he retired in 2000, and he finished with 260 goals and 441 points in 608 games as a Maple Leaf. He also added 34 goals and 61 points in 79 playoff games with Toronto. He now works for the Leafs as a community representative. Clark is still one of the most popular Leafs of all time and was named as one of the top 25 players in team history.

ABOUT WAYNE GRETZKY

Wayne Gretzky was born in Brantford, Ontario in 1961. In the 1971–72 season, he scored 378 goals and recorded 139 assists in 85 games while playing in his hometown. By the age of 17 he was playing professional hockey in the World Hockey Association, and he made it to the NHL when the Edmonton Oilers joined the league in 1979. Edmonton traded him to the Los Angeles Kings in 1988. He won four Stanley Cups with the Oilers and took the Art Ross Trophy (as the NHL's leading scorer) 10 times. He also won the Lady Byng Trophy (for gentlemanly play) five times and the Conn Smythe (as best player in playoffs) twice. He finished his remarkable career holding 61 NHL records, including most career goals (894), assists (1,963) and points (2,857). Gretzky also holds the career marks for most goals (122), assists (260) and points (382) in the playoffs. On his performance in the seventh game against the Maple Leafs in the 1993 playoffs, Gretzky later said, "In my estimation, that was the best game I played in the NHL." Gretzky is now head coach and part-owner of the Phoenix Coyotes.